Elephant's Graveyard
Abridged Version

by George Brant

A SAMUEL FRENCH ACTING EDITION

NEW YORK HOLLYWOOD LONDON TORONTO

SAMUELFRENCH.COM

Copyright © 2010 by George Brant

ALL RIGHTS RESERVED

Cover Art by Nik Perleros with Balagan Theatre

ISBN 978-0-573-69837-8   Printed in U.S.A.   #29649

MUSIC USE NOTE

Licensees are solely responsible for obtaining formal written permission from copyright owners to use copyrighted music in the performance of this play and are strongly cautioned to do so. If no such permission is obtained by the licensee, then the licensee must use only original music that the licensee owns and controls. Licensees are solely responsible and liable for all music clearances and shall indemnify the copyright owners of the play and their licensing agent, Samuel French, Inc., against any costs, expenses, losses and liabilities arising from the use of music by licensees.

IMPORTANT BILLING AND CREDIT
REQUIREMENTS

All producers of *ELEPHANT'S GRAVEYARD - ABRIDGED VERSION* must give credit to the Author of the Play in all programs distributed in connection with performances of the Play, and in all instances in which the title of the Play appears for the purposes of advertising, publicizing or otherwise exploiting the Play and/or a production. The name of the Author *must* appear on a separate line on which no other name appears, immediately following the title and *must* appear in size of type not less than fifty percent of the size of the title type.

In addition the following credit *must* be given in all programs and publicity information distributed in association with this piece:

Originally produced by Trustus Theatre, Columbia, South Carolina.
Jim Thigpen, Artistic Director.

ELEPHANT'S GRAVEYARD was first produced by the University of Texas at Austin in the Oscar Brockett Theatre in Austin, Texas on November 16, 2007. The performance was directed by Laura Kepley, with sets by Szu-Feng Chen, costumes by Jan McCauley, lighting by Jennifer Madison, dramaturgy by Erica Nagel. The production stage manager was Lori Grubbs. The cast was as follows:

PREACHER	Neil Ames
GUITARIST	James Betz
MUDDY TOWNSPERSON	Lizzi Biggers
HUNGRY TOWNSPERSON	Matrex Kilgore
STEAM SHOVEL OPERATOR	Daniel Salmones
YOUNG TOWNSPERSON	Shannon Schaefer
MARSHAL	Tom Truss
RINGMASTER	George Brant
BALLET GIRL	Anna Fugate
TRAINER	Tim Longo
CLOWN	Ben Schave
STRONGMAN	Hunter Smith
DRUMMER	Mark Smoot
TOUR MANAGER	Shaun Tubbs
ENGINEER	Keenan Zarling

ELEPHANT'S GRAVEYARD had its non-equity premiere at the Trustus Theatre in Columbia, South Carolina on May 1, 2009. The performance was directed by Robert Richmond, sound by Baxter Engle, with sets by Samantha Hayford, costumes by Valerie Pruett, lighting by Joe Laney. The production stage manager was Taylor Harrison. The cast was as follows:

RINGMASTER	Michael Downey
TRAINER	Steven Kopp
BALLET GIRL	Vicky Saye Henderson
TOUR MANAGER	Gary Pozsik
STRONGMAN	Will Moreau
CLOWN	Alec Grooms
HUNGRY TOWNSPERSON	Jabar K. Hankins
MARSHAL	Scott Stepp
MUDDY TOWNSPERSON	Robin Gottlieb
PREACHER	Alex Smith
STEAM SHOVEL OPERATOR	Bobby Bloom
YOUNG TOWNSPERSON	Mary Tilden
GUITARIST	Leisl Downey
ENGINEER	Jonathan Jackson

ELEPHANT'S GRAVEYARD was the winner of the 2008 Keene Prize for Literature and 2008 David Mark Cohen National Playwriting Award

CHARACTERS

The Circus

RINGMASTER – obsessed with the bottom line

TRAINER – loves his work

BALLET GIRL – a showgirl in control

TOUR MANAGER – bit of a bully

STRONGMAN – a proud muscleman from Europe's far-off shores

CLOWN – a comedian with an inferiority complex

DRUMMER (optional) – keeps the beat

The Town

HUNGRY TOWNSPERSON – African-American, a steel-trap memory

MARSHAL – keeps the peace

MUDDY TOWNSPERSON – a haunted widow

PREACHER – doggedly hopeful

STEAM SHOVEL OPERATOR – looking for escape

YOUNG TOWNSPERSON – excitable dreamer

GUITARIST/HARMONICA PLAYER (optional) – sets the rhythm

The Railroad

ENGINEER – confident Time is on his side

AUTHOR'S NOTES

Sound

All music and sound effects should be provided live by the Drummer and Guitarist (drum rolls, gunshots, train whistles, etc.). The Drummer is primarily an instrument of the Circus; the Guitarist is primarily an instrument of the Town.

Set

The set may be an empty stage or an abstract collision of the worlds of the Circus, Town and Railroad. This collision need not be pretty.

Performance

The telling of this story must be active, a sort of present past, allowing for a full range of emotion; the end must not be played at the beginning.

Staging

If an action is described by the storytellers, it should not be shown. The staging of the play should complement the dialogue, not make it redundant.

Casting

Roles may be played by any race or gender except when specified.

Version

Please note this is the abridged version of the script. The full-length version is also available from Samuel French.

Special Thanks

Marla Akin, ATHE, Balagan Theatre, Chris Benson, Stephen Berenson, the Brants, Mark Charney, Sheila Daniels, Ron Daniels, Steven Dietz, Michael Evenden, Jake Groshong, Jason Harber, Gregg Henry, Daniel Alexander Jones, E.L. Keene, the Kennedy Center, Caitlin MacLeod, James Magnuson, Denise Martel, Emily Morse, Erica Nagel, Charles Otte, Daniel Patterson, Charles Edwin Price, Robert Richmond, Judith Royer, Kate Snodgrass, Jim and Kay Thigpen, Adrienne Thompson, Trinity Repertory Company, Trustus Theatre, Jon Tuttle, Naomi Wallace, Craig Watson, David White, Dawn Youngs, Suzan Zeder, all the casts, crews, and designers who have worked on the play and my first and best reader, Laura Kepley.

Development

Elephant's Graveyard was developed with the generous assistance of the James A. Michener Center for Writers, The University of Texas at Austin, and WordBRIDGE Playwright's Lab.

"Friday I tasted life. It was a vast morsel. A Circus passed the house – still I feel the red in my mind though the drums are out."

– Emily Dickinson

For Mary

(A drum roll summons the characters from the darkness. The drums crescendo and end with a flourish.)

HUNGRY TOWNSPERSON. It was September and there was a Town

ALL TOWNSPEOPLE. Erwin, Tennessee

BALLET GIRL. There was a Circus

RINGMASTER. Sparks World Famous Shows Proudly Presents –

STEAM SHOVEL OPERATOR. There was a Railroad

ENGINEER. The Clinchfield and Ohio

YOUNG TOWNSPERSON. There was an Elephant

ALL CIRCUS. Mary

ALL TOWNSPEOPLE. Mary

ALL. Mary

TOUR MANAGER. And there was a Man with Red Hair.

(A train whistle.)

ENGINEER. It was September and there was a Town and a Circus.

RINGMASTER. Charlie Sparks. Owner, operator. Sparks World Famous Shows.

You want to run a circus? Always keep it about the money.

Oh, you might have a dream – a dream of making a crowd leap to its feet, clamor with one voice, "Sparks, Sparks, Sparks!"

But be careful. You're the Ringmaster. Dreams aren't for you. Dreams are for rubbernecks. Dreams are for suckers.

*(The **HUNGRY TOWNSPERSON** eats from a bag of peanuts, as he does throughout the play.)*

HUNGRY TOWNSPERSON. Erwin. The town that couldn't remember its own name. True story. S'posed to be named Er-*vin* after some rich fella. Postmaster messed up, spelled it E-r-w-i-n instead. Nobody remembered to fix it.

Yep.

That's Erwin for you.

STRONGMAN. I lift things.

Heavy things.

Anything.

This gets me on boat.

This gets me to America.

This gets me to Circus.

STEAM SHOVEL OPERATOR. Never been nowhere.
Work a steam shovel down at Erwin railyard. Dig holes all day.

One…hole…after…another.

Papers say we might go to war with the Kaiser? I'll be the first to sign up.

"Oo-ee, what a patriotic young man."

Hell.

Ain't patriotic. Just bored.

(A drum roll building to cymbal crash as lights up on…)

BALLET GIRL. Ballet Girl.

(She strikes a fetching pose to a tinkling of cymbal.)
Ballet Girl.

(Another pose and cymbal.)
Ballet Girl.

(Another, to a cymbal crash, then rude drum thump.)
Can't dance. Practically old enough to have a girl of my own. But Ballet Girl it is.

Not a show girl, a Ballet Girl. Substitute "ballet" for "show" and I'm not a scandal; I'm an artist. I'm not a temptress in tights; I'm a dancer.

A Ballet Girl. That's me. From head to toe.

MUDDY TOWNSPERSON. Mud.

Yella mud.

Everywhere.

Boardwalks help some. Not enough.

Always scrapin' it off yer shoes.

Enough to drive a person crazy, all that scrapin'.

Buried two kids in the mud…husband. Mud tryin' to swallow me up, swallow this whole town up. God's punishin' us for somethin'. Take another flood to wash Erwin clean.

PREACHER. I finished puttin' up the Erwin Evergreen Free Will Church in July. Turns out I mighta been a bit optimistic about how many rows of pews I needed. Little quiet on Sundays.

Love…forgiveness…joy.

I'll keep on testifyin', but…there's nothin' more lonely than a New Testament preacher in an Old Testament town.

TRAINER. It's love.
Feed her, wash her, sleep with her. Hell, end of the day, I even have a drink with her. Pour some whiskey in her bucket, mix it with some water – she loves it. Sticks her trunk in, it's gone in a second.
I'm lucky. They live a long time. You play your cards right, you got a friend for life.

YOUNG TOWNSPERSON. Could use more friends, I guess.
Play with my brother Eli.

Skip stones at trains.

Read Tarzan books! He's somethin'. Read 'em right before bed. Gives me the best dreams.

(The **CLOWN** *enters, performs his routine to drum accompaniment. At its conclusion, he waits for applause, laughter. Nothing. He dismisses the audience.)*

CLOWN. Too old, the lot of ya. *(the* **YOUNG TOWNSPERSON***)* Kids laugh. Easy peasie.

And we joeys give kids more than laughs. Give 'em perspective, a lesson to carry forever, biggie: that there's always someone worse off than you.

(A "ba-dooom-ching" from the drums.)

Except for us. Nothin' below a clown. They all pull rank, even the ballet girls. We're the last ones to get the make-up mirror – even though we use the most make-up.

("Ba-doom-ching.")

Let me put it this way: How many Ringmasters does it take to change a lightbulb? None. They tell the clowns to do it.

("Ba-doom-ching.")

MARSHAL. Erwin. Risin' taller every year. Best this country has to offer.

Peaceful. Keep it that way.

Folks 'round here honest, law abidin'.

Ain't the folks 'round here I worry 'bout. It's the strangers. It's that damn train station.

TOUR MANAGER. All the travelin' from town to town – all the firin', hirin': me.

Firin' happens all the time. Fella's lucky: he gets fired in one of the towns during a stop. Unlucky: he gets redlighted: tossed off our train while it's movin'. Sucker don't see nothin' but the red lights of the caboose as it fades away.

And hirin'. Yeah. Do a lot o' that, too. Circus needs plenty of muscle – and not just in the ring. Townies get out of line now and then – want to prove they're tougher than the Strongman, get fresh with a ballet girl. Sparks sees any funny business, he calls out the "Hey Rube." I gotta teach every new hire: they hear that "Hey Rube," they drop whatever they're doin' and defend their own.

(A train whistle sounds.)

MUDDY TOWNSPERSON. It was September and there was a Town and a Circus and a Railroad.

ENGINEER. The Railroad invented Time in America. We came along and told this country: we have a schedule to keep. Time is not relative; Time is precise. Time is not grey; it is black and white.

The Circus, Erwin, they have our guarantee:

You can depend on the Railroad.

(The train whistle sounds.)

HUNGRY TOWNSPERSON. It was September and there was a Town

RINGMASTER. There was a Circus

ENGINEER. There was a Railroad

TRAINER. And there was an Elephant.

HUNGRY TOWNSPERSON. Mary

YOUNG TOWNSPERSON. We dreamed her before we saw her

MUDDY TOWNSPERSON. She was plastered on every telephone pole

STEAM SHOVEL OPERATOR. Every fence post

MARSHAL. Every barn door

PREACHER. September

YOUNG TOWNSPERSON. The Circus was coming

HUNGRY TOWNSPERSON. She was coming

MUDDY TOWNSPERSON. To our muddy town

MARSHAL. It was all there in black and white

STEAM SHOVEL OPERATOR. And color

PREACHER. It said:

(Drum roll takes over as the Circus embodies the Sparks poster.)

RINGMASTER. Ladies and Gentlemen, Children of All Ages, Sparks World Famous Shows

The Show that Never Broke a Promise

BALLET GIRL. Moral, entertaining, instructive

TOUR MANAGER. Twenty-five years of honest dealing with the public

STRONGMAN. Proudly presents a tremendous exhibition of wealth and splendor

CLOWN. All new for 1916

TRAINER. Starring Mary: the largest living land animal on Earth

STRONGMAN. Death–defying feats of skill and daring

BALLET GIRL. Mary: over five tons

TOUR MANAGER. Two packs of man-killing lions

STRONGMAN. Mary: three inches taller than Jumbo

TOUR MANAGER. Five thousand seats

RINGMASTER. Mary: guaranteed at every performance

TRAINER. A free street parade each day at noon

CLOWN. Mary

TOUR MANAGER. Mary

STRONGMAN. Mary

BALLET GIRL. Mary

TRAINER. Mary

ALL. Mary

Mary

Mary

Mary

Mary

Mary

RINGMASTER. An elephant is an investment.

You open up your pocketbook, you throw down the eight grand, don't think about it again. Simple.

You've got the trained seals, the trapeze, the Strong-man. Fine, but they aren't the bread and butter. No rubberneck comes to a circus doesn't have an ele-phant. Strike that. No rubberneck comes to a circus doesn't have a *big* elephant.

TRAINER. They love a parade. All elephants do in the wild anyway, walk around. Wild elephant herd follows the leader and the leader is the biggest female. I got no reason to mess with that here.

So, they all march behind Mary. Shadrack, Penny, Sue, little Mabel, one behind the other, trunk wrapped around the tail in front of her.

Let me tell ya, only thing better than watchin' an ele-phant parade is bein' in the elephant parade. Only thing better than bein' in the elephant parade is leadin' it. A dream. Sittin' on top of the world – little Shorty – on top of my own personal mountain, on top of Mary, legs wrapped around her back, head in the clouds.

(Drum roll. The **STRONGMAN***'s entire body trembles as he holds a heavily weighted barbell over his head. Cymbal crash.)*

STRONGMAN. Impressive, no? No?

So tell me.

I do not cost as much.

I am not as temperamental.

I do not relieve myself all over the stage.

So tell me – please – have the courtesy to inform me:

Why is that elephant the star of the show?

(Drum roll, cymbal crash. The **BALLET GIRL** *strikes a pose as if she's in Mary's trunk.)*

BALLET GIRL. Once I'm decreed safe, nothing more than a wholesome Ballet Girl, then...I add the elephant.

Five tons of grey flesh bearing me half-naked into the ring, wrapped up tightly in its trunk.

Oh, I'm never more powerful, sensual, dangerous, than when I'm with Mary. Keep your spangles, your makeup, your headdress. Diamonds? Diamonds are nothing. An elephant is a girl's best friend.

TOUR MANAGER. They're the hardest workers I got. They load and unload the boxcars, push up the tent poles… those tuskers can do anything.

CLOWN. *(juggling)* Nobody looks down on the elephants. Right? They don't have to put on make-up or play the dope to get applause. They're too mighty to ever be made humble, too strong to ever be broken, too big to ever be laid low.

And Mary's the biggest we joeys've ever seen. So we love her the most.

RINGMASTER. Listen.

An elephant isn't cute, isn't a friend, isn't a symbol for something else. An elephant is an elephant.

And an elephant is an investment.

(Train whistle.)

CLOWN. *(counting on fingers)* It was September and there was a Town and there was a Circus and there was a Railroad and there was an Elephant and…ah! Last but not least…there was a Man with Red Hair.

TRAINER. Lou knocks on my boxcar, tells me I got a new roommate. Goofy-lookin' red-haired guy. I tell Lou, crowded enough in here with five elephants, but he insists. Tells me Red's my new partner.

Don't like partners.

But I'm not gonna be a jerk about it. I show Red his corner. He gripes about the smell and I tell him get used to it. Townies think elephants smell bad in the ring, try sleepin' with one in a boxcar. He shuts up when he sees Mary, looks at her like she's the answer to his prayers.

I don't know what's wrong with the guy – if he's a nut or soft in the head or what. Any case, I ain't gonna turn my back on him. I may not be big, but…if he makes one wrong move, Red's gettin' the red-light.

(A train whistle.)

ENGINEER. Click-clack click-clack through the night.

Erwin is waiting and we will not disappoint.

You can depend on the Railroad.

STEAM SHOVEL OPERATOR. Dig.

Dig.

Dig.

Dig.

Dig.

Dig.

(The sound of the circus train approaching.)

Train.

Whistle.

Elephant.

(He smiles.)

Circus!

(The Circus folk transform the space in some fashion, creating a sense of the Big Top arriving.)

YOUNG TOWNSPERSON. Eli woke me up at 4:00 a.m.

I cussed him out – thought we was gonna be late.

Peeped in at our folks, still sleepin'. Snuck out the window, ran as fast as we could to the field where they'd do it.

We were all there, all the kids in Erwin, there to watch 'em set up the Big Top. The Greatest Free Show on Earth.

Train whistled, brakes screamed, men and animals stomped outta every door. Everybody marched around, seemed to know what they're doin' 'cept this

YOUNG TOWNSPERSON. *(cont.)* red-haired guy…he kept bumpin' into stuff, trippin' on ropes. People yelled at him and his face turned as red as his hair.

Then this elephant came out…I 'bout peed myself. It made this big trumpet? We 'bout peed ourselves.

The men unloaded the main tent pole and set it right between that thing's eyes. It walked on forward – boom, boom, boom – pushin' the pole up in the air as it stomped: higher, higher, higher.
Was like a dream.

That's 'bout my favorite parta the circus. Watchin' 'em set up. That and the parade.

Was really lookin' forward to that parade.

MARSHAL. 'Bout nine a.m. Ringmaster cleared the route with me. Told me to keep the horses away. Could spook the elephants.

Yes sir, yes sir, whatever you want, sir. Main Street will hold its horses.

Hell.

Not enough I gotta let the circus come to town and pick the pockets of all'a us. I got to roll out the red carpet for 'em while they do it.

TRAINER. I'd shown Red how to feed her, groom her, that's it. That's all he knew. Lou waltzed in – says,

TOUR MANAGER. Big deal Shorty, Red wants to ride Mary in the march. Back off and give the new guy a chance.

TRAINER. I shoulda said no. I shoulda told Lou she was mine.

TOUR MANAGER. He didn't say nothin'.

TRAINER. I didn't say nothin'. Just stepped aside. Maybe made a face. That was my big protest, a face.

TOUR MANAGER. *(laughing)* The kisser on that guy.

TRAINER. It's trust. Trust you build up over years, not one day. Every peanut, every bath, every pat on the trunk.

It's trust. Love.

But Red didn't have time for any of that. Red had a parade to lead.

RINGMASTER. Shorty's on Shadrack, but he still has to make the call – they won't start walkin' for anyone but him.

(The **RINGMASTER** *gestures to the* **TRAINER** *to start the parade.)*

TRAINER. TRUNKS UP!

(Circus music as the parade begins.)

PREACHER. I opened the doors and the steps to the church were thick with people. Faces I'd never seen before. I was fixin' to thank Jesus for answerin' my prayers.

People weren't tryin' to get in, though. Steps were just the best place to face *out.* To see the parade. Provided a little height.

All there. Whole town was linin' the street: white, colored, man, woman, child, all there. Glow in their eyes, waitin' to see a miracle.

Well. If I couldn't provide that glow on Sundays…at least there was something that could.

(The next sequence spoken slowly, in awe and joy, as the parade passes in front of the Townspeople.)

MUDDY TOWNSPERSON. Right down Main Street. Our Main Street.

STEAM SHOVEL OPERATOR. Had the day off from the shovel. Everybody had the day off. Circus Day.

YOUNG TOWNSPERSON. Eli and I 'bout peed ourselves.

MUDDY TOWNSPERSON. Elephants, clowns, tigers…all muckin' down our Main Street. Through our yella mud.

STEAM SHOVEL OPERATOR. Made Erwin look like somethin' for once.

YOUNG TOWNSPERSON. Could hear the brass band and bass drum for miles.

MUDDY TOWNSPERSON. Mud on alla them circus folk. Hems of their dresses, tails of their coats.

STEAM SHOVEL OPERATOR. Colors you never dreamed of.

YOUNG TOWNSPERSON. So long. Stretched on forever.

MUDDY TOWNSPERSON. Elephant had Erwin mud all over it.

STEAM SHOVEL OPERATOR. Our yella town gone all purple and silver and red.

YOUNG TOWNSPERSON. That big elephant was leadin' the whole thing. That goofy guy – red hair? He was up on her back.

ALL TOWNSPEOPLE. Mary

Mary

Mary

Mary!

HUNGRY TOWNSPERSON. And then? Well, then the dominoes start to fallin':

Elephant sees melon.

Elephant walks toward melon.

Elephant rider turns red.

Elephant rider encourages elephant to abandon melon.

Elephant ignores elephant rider.

Elephant rider is most insistent, to the tune of elephant hook across elephant head.

Elephant keeps walkin' toward melon.

Elephant holds up parade.

Elephant rider turns red.

Elephant rider breaks elephant hook across elephant tusk.

Elephant thinks.

Elephant decides she's had enough of elephant rider.

Elephant picks elephant rider off elephant back with elephant trunk.

Elephant trunk throws elephant rider into soda pop stand.

Elephant rider groans in rubble.

Elephant rider thinks it's over.

Elephant rider is wrong.

Elephant walks over to elephant rider and puts elephant foot on elephant rider head.

Elephant rider screams.

Elephant foot steps…on…down.

Elephant rider head explodes like a melon.

Elephant rider turns red.

Elephant walks away.

Elephant rider don't.

Elephant, free of elephant rider, strolls on over and helps herself to some melon.

Simple.

Parade stops, man dies, elephant turns killer. All for a melon.

(Chaos and screams as we re-enter "real-time." A gunshot. Several gunshots.)

MARSHAL. Nothin'. Thing didn't flinch.

Somebody screamed. Townsfolk ran off in a panic.

Couldn't do nothin' but stand there holdin' my empty pop gun.

And that thing kept eatin' the melon, rippin' apart its little snack while that poor man's crushed head sat next to it, all opened up and leakin'.

The Ringmaster ran up and told me we'll settle this later. I told him yes we will. Then a little guy led that thing back to the fairgrounds while some carnies carted the leakin' fella off in one of them animal cages. Clowns washed the street down with buckets of water. Vanished.

Quiet for a minute, like nothin' happened.

Townsfolk came back.

Most of 'em were cryin'.

A few were laughin'. At me.

PREACHER. Folks lined up again three deep on the street, waitin' for someone to tell 'em what to do. I propped the church doors open, but no one came in.

STEAM SHOVEL OPERATOR. There was a pool of blood and brains in front of the post office.

YOUNG TOWNSPERSON. I heard his head crack open again. In *my* head. Sharp crack, then softer ones, one after 'nother. CRACK crack crack crack CRACK crack crack crack –

MUDDY TOWNSPERSON. She stepped on his skull. Crushed it. Sent another body into the mud.

PREACHER. No one came in.

STEAM SHOVEL OPERATOR. Couldn't stop lookin' at that blood.

YOUNG TOWNSPERSON. CRACK crack crack crack

MUDDY TOWNSPERSON. Town's cursed.

PREACHER. No one.

STEAM SHOVEL OPERATOR. Heard that fella was from Kingsport.

YOUNG TOWNSPERSON. Eli thought he knew him.

MUDDY TOWNSPERSON. Coulda been any of us.

PREACHER. No one.

STEAM SHOVEL OPERATOR. Carl said she killed two men in Virginia

MUDDY TOWNSPERSON. Seven men

YOUNG TOWNSPERSON. Eighteen

ALL TOWNSPEOPLE. Right on Main Street

STEAM SHOVEL OPERATOR. It can't just do that. Can it? Go 'round killin' people?

ALL TOWNSPEOPLE. Our Main Street

YOUNG TOWNSPERSON. Tarzan woulda stopped her. Tarzan woulda jumped on her back and stabbed her through the eyes and gouged out her brain.

ALL TOWNSPEOPLE. Right on Main Street.

MUDDY TOWNSPERSON. Eye for an eye. Eye for an eye and maybe God'll stop punishin' us.

ALL TOWNSPEOPLE. Our Main Street

(The following lines are spoken simultaneously and loudly.)

HUNGRY TOWNSPERSON. All for the want of a hog. All for the want of a hog.

PREACHER. No one comes in. No one comes in.

MARSHAL. A few are laughin'. At me. A few are laughin'. At me.

YOUNG TOWNSPERSON. That's what Tarzan woulda done. That's what Tarzan woulda done.

MUDDY TOWNSPERSON. Eye for an eye. Eye for an eye and God'll stop punishin' us.

STEAM SHOVEL OPERATOR. It can't just do that. Can it? It can't just do that. Can it?

(The simultaneous speech moves into –)

ALL TOWNSPEOPLE. Right on Main Street
Our Main Street
Right on Main Street
Our Main Street
Right on Main Street
Our.....

*(The **MARSHAL** rises above the crowd.)*

MARSHAL. It coulda ended there, but that wouldn'ta been right, that wouldn'ta been justice. Maybe my pistol didn't mean squat to that thing, but damnit, we'd find something that would. It wasn't walking away from this.

Erwin don't look kindly upon murderers.

HUNGRY TOWNSPERSON. Crowd breaks up and follows the Marshal into the saloon. I stand in the doorway. Hear talk, lots of talk. Talk about public menace, talk about what you do with rabid dogs, talk about what's right and wrong.

PREACHER. I stared at the steps. The empty steps. I walked into the church and let the doors swing shut behind me.

TOUR MANAGER. Tried to get in touch with Red's family, friends. Didn't have none.

TRAINER. Like he didn't exist except for us, like he was born to do nothin' but cause us trouble.

BALLET GIRL. Poor kid.

STRONGMAN. He was weak.

Did not understand.

You are on top of her, but she is strong one.

Not you.

CLOWN. Us joeys said a few words and buried 'im at the fairground.

RINGMASTER. You still have a show to do that night. Must go on.

DOORS!

(The Townspeople enter the Big Top. They are dimly lit, indistinguishable, threatening.)

TOUR MANAGER. I told Charlie, maybe we should keep Mary out, maybe the people'd forget. But he told me what I already knew:

RINGMASTER. They won't forget. Aren't coming to see the circus. Coming to see the killer.

TOUR MANAGER. He was right. Woulda been a riot if we kept her away.

*(Drum roll, spotlight on the **RINGMASTER**.)*

RINGMASTER. Ladies and Gentlemen, Children of All Ages, Sparks World Famous Shows Proudly Presents –

TOUR MANAGER. Normal night we play up the danger, talk up the toothless tiger. Not this time. Ballet Girl brought Mary out like she was the most innocent a' God's creatures.

BALLET GIRL. Look at me, all of you. Here I am, all wrapped up, cuddled up in the very trunk that did the deed, and am I scared, am I trembling?

I am smiling. Smiling!

TOUR MANAGER. But it didn't work. Those people weren't there to forgive. They stood up and pelted her with popcorn. And then they made this sound....

RINGMASTER. Listen to that.

It comes true. Your dream comes true. In a tiny town in Tennessee. Crowd leaps to its feet and speaks with one voice, shakes the air, makes it tremble.

It's not the "Sparks, Sparks, Sparks," you dreamed of, but, oh…they scream 'till their lungs ache, louder than any lion's roar. Young and old united in one glorious moment of certainty. Their scream, their chant, their heart's greatest wish:

"Kill it. Kill it. Kill it."

(The Drummer creates a continuous threatening pulse throughout the rest of the Big Top section, a pulse that sometimes explodes into loud bursts of sound.)

YOUNG TOWNSPERSON. It got louder. The Marshal and people were wavin' guns around. Everybody shoutin'. All 'cept the colored section.

HUNGRY TOWNSPERSON. No need to say nothin'. Erwin don't give you no vote. Best to keep your mouth shut.

YOUNG TOWNSPERSON. Then the clown started talkin'. Never knew clowns could talk.

CLOWN. No, no, no! Red was one of us. Part of the circus. He knew the risks!

YOUNG TOWNSPERSON. This little guy came out –

TRAINER. You all saw him hittin' her tusk with the hook! What's she s'posed to do? She stopped him, that's all. She stopped him!

YOUNG TOWNSPERSON. The Marshal and the new Preacher stood up –

MARSHAL. These carnies can talk all they want. We know what we seen. And the People of Erwin demand –

PREACHER. No.

No, we don't.

PREACHER. *(cont.)* I didn't cast no vote. No vote was counted.

I'm a person, God knows. But I'm not, I'm not the People. I'm not the –

MARSHAL. We know what we seen.

And the People, the People of Erwin demand justice.

YOUNG TOWNSPERSON. Louder! Then the Strongman grabbed a barbell and started shoutin' at the Ringmaster –

STRONGMAN. Sparks! Call the Hey Rube! Call it! Sparks!

YOUNG TOWNSPERSON. But the Ringmaster didn't do nothin'.

STRONGMAN. Let loose the tigers, the lions! The rubbernecks want to know who is stronger? Their puny chests, their straw hats – I will crush them all! Sparks! Call the Hey Rube! Sparks! Call it! Sparks!

YOUNG TOWNSPERSON. Fin'ly the Ringmaster raised his hand –

(The **RINGMASTER** *raises his hand.)*

And everything got quiet.

(It does. The **RINGMASTER** *speaks privately to us.)*

RINGMASTER. Now, eight thousand dollars is a lot to lose. A lot to lose in a hick town middle of nowhere.

But investments get tricky when the people want blood.

Because it's not just Erwin. Your advance men wire back from your upcoming stops: Johnson City, Rogersville, Indian Ridge: your circus isn't welcome until that elephant is taken care of.

So.

Is she still worth eight thousand?

Is she still worth anything?

(Spotlight on the **RINGMASTER.***)*

Ladies and Gentlemen, Children of All Ages – the Circus Understands. The Circus Understands Your

Wishes. This Mary Matter Will Be Settled to Your Liking Tomorrow. And…and We are Open to Suggestions.

ENGINEER. The Marshal knew shooting it with a pistol hadn't worked, so they talked about getting a cannon, a Civil War cannon from the nearby museum.

They talked about electrocuting it, frying it like some of them had seen in the moving picture Thomas Edison made. But that was copycat stuff, that wasn't dreaming big enough.

We had the answer. We always have the answer.

The railyard. There's a crane there can lift 100 tons. Says so on the side of it, right there in black and white. Nothing grey can stand up to that much black and white. Now, something like that could do something special, something never been done before. Why, something like that could hang her. Hang her like any other murderer. She may be big, but that Railroad crane's bigger. Crane'll get the job done. Crane'll do the trick. Crane's the Railroad, after all.

And you can always depend on the Railroad.

(The Townspeople disperse, heading home for the night.)

MARSHAL. Hangin' suits me fine, I guess.
Still think the cannon would be better.

MUDDY TOWNSPERSON. Eye for an eye. Erwin'll fin'ly be clean.

STEAM SHOVEL OPERATOR. I'd'a never believed it. Erwin. Erwin is the place to be tomorrow. Ain't nobody else – I mean nobody – nobody else in the world is hangin' an elephant tomorrow.

So that's somethin'.

That's somethin' *we* got.

You want to see it, you get off your fat butt and come here for a change.

(The Townspeople are gone.)

TRAINER. So now Lou and Sparks need my help.

What am I gonna do?

Walk away, leave 'em to figure this out themselves?

No.

I stay.

I stay 'cause if I don't, they'll mess it up. It'll be even worse of a spectacle.

Lou and Sparks are happy this is my answer. Smile and open their mouths.

I stop 'em.

I tell 'em, don't think I've forgiven you. Don't think that. I will never forgive you.

But I tell 'em, go ahead, what's your question?

They ask how to get her out to the railyard tomorrow, how to lead her through all those people without all Hell breakin' loose.

I think.

I tell 'em.

Tuskers aren't stupid, they know when somethin's up. You have to make her think it's a normal march. She can't go out there alone.

Mary has to lead the parade, like it's any other parade. Shadrack, Penny, Sue, little Mabel, all of 'em. Walkin' trunk-to-tail like always.

Then what?

Then this.

Then chain Mary's foot to the track under the crane so she can't move. Then Lou, you lead the rest of the elephants away, fast, before they smell the panic on her. Then somebody runs up Mary's back and puts the hangin' chain 'round her neck. Someone she knows, someone she trusts.

They look at me like I'm crazy.

I tell them to relax.

I tell them I'll do it.

RINGMASTER. You don't sleep that night.

You think.

You wish you could charge admission tomorrow, but… this isn't your show.

It's theirs.

(The Townspeople transform the space in some way over the following, making it theirs. They also add items of clothing such as a parasol or a more formal hat to their attire. The Circus folk do the opposite, exchanging their flashy costumes for a more muted look. The **ENGINEER** *remains the same.)*

MUDDY TOWNSPERSON. Mornin' fin'ly came.

HUNGRY TOWNSPERSON. Couldn't help but feel it – there was a spark in the air.

MUDDY TOWNSPERSON. Put on brand new shoes. Wanted to look my best.

YOUNG TOWNSPERSON. Ma told us not to go. But Eli and me? We was goin'.

MUDDY TOWNSPERSON. Got to the railroad tracks, saw I wasn't the only one gussied up.

PREACHER. I went to bear witness. To see the glow.

MUDDY TOWNSPERSON. Men in the only suits they owned. Women in their Sunday best, prancin' around with parasols like it was Easter.

MARSHAL. Never been so proud.

MUDDY TOWNSPERSON. All'a Erwin. Seemed like all'a Tennessee.

HUNGRY TOWNSPERSON. Quite a sight.

MUDDY TOWNSPERSON. People risin' outta the mud, standin' top of boxcars, top of cranes, coal tipples.

STEAM SHOVEL OPERATOR. Was sittin' in the cab of my steam shovel. Best seat in the house.

MUDDY TOWNSPERSON. Picnic baskets, food, punch.

MARSHAL. We were doin' it up right.

MUDDY TOWNSPERSON. Everybody was sharin' with everybody else.

HUNGRY TOWNSPERSON. I kept to myself.

MUDDY TOWNSPERSON. Laughin', dancin'.

PREACHER. Glow was brighter than the sun.

MUDDY TOWNSPERSON. All the kids were play-actin' what was gonna happen.

YOUNG TOWNSPERSON. Eli and me were 'bout peein' ourselves.

MUDDY TOWNSPERSON. Saw some men drinkin'.

STEAM SHOVEL OPERATOR. I saw Carl and them havin' a good ole time down there behind a caboose.

MUDDY TOWNSPERSON. I took the bottle outta their hands, smashed it on the tracks. They looked at me like I was crazy. But I knew it was wrong. Wrong to sully the act with liquor.

MARSHAL. It was gonna be somethin'.

MUDDY TOWNSPERSON. Act had to be pure, clean.

YOUNG TOWNSPERSON. I couldn't take it no more.

MUDDY TOWNSPERSON. You could feel it – we were ready.

RINGMASTER. You wait for the signal from Johnny Tin Plate.

(*The* **MARSHAL** *draws his pistol and fires it into the air.*)

RINGMASTER. You tell Shorty to go 'head.

(*The* **RINGMASTER** *gestures to the* **TRAINER** *to start the parade.*)

TRAINER. TRUNKS UP!

(*Marching drums.*)

STEAM SHOVEL OPERATOR. The killer was in front. Them elephants marched out holdin' each other's tails with their trunks – like a parade or a line of boxcars.

MARSHAL. Why they hell did they bring those other ones out?

STEAM SHOVEL OPERATOR. They walked all through the railyard up to the crane and this short guy chained the killer's foot to a train track.

TRAINER. *(under his breath)* Now, Lou, now!

TOUR MANAGER. I grabbed Shadrack.

YOUNG TOWNSPERSON. Then the elephants started makin' this sound. Like they knew once they left, the big one was gonna get it.

TRAINER. *(under his breath)* Get them out!

YOUNG TOWNSPERSON. Real funny sound.

TRAINER. *(under his breath)* Now!

YOUNG TOWNSPERSON. Sounded kinda human.

PREACHER. Lord.

YOUNG TOWNSPERSON. Like 20, 30 people moanin' full out at the same time.

TOUR MANAGER. C'mon! C'mon!

YOUNG TOWNSPERSON. Eli and me plugged our ears.

TOUR MANAGER. Finally got Shadrack and the rest of 'em outta sight.

MARSHAL. Finally.

YOUNG TOWNSPERSON. We took our fingers out.

TRAINER. *(calming Mary down)* It's okay, it's okay, it's okay. Ready?
Showtime, sweetie.

STEAM SHOVEL OPERATOR. Short guy ran up her back.

MARSHAL. The women were hidin' their faces, or pretendin' to.

YOUNG TOWNSPERSON. We was 'fraid she was gonna pick him up with her trunk like she did that red-haired fella.

STEAM SHOVEL OPERATOR. But she didn't seem spooked at all. The short guy hooked the chain 'round her neck, patted her back and stood up.

(The Townspeople applaud.)

PREACHER. The little man ran off and she was alone.

MUDDY TOWNSPERSON. Mud in between the folds of her skin.

YOUNG TOWNSPERSON. She looked scary.

PREACHER. Helpless.

STEAM SHOVEL OPERATOR. Confused.

MUDDY TOWNSPERSON. Guilty.

MARSHAL. Like a killer.

HUNGRY TOWNSPERSON. Like a queen.

YOUNG TOWNSPERSON. The Marshal looked up at the Engineer and –

(The **MARSHAL** *fires his pistol into the air once more.)*

ENGINEER. Time.

The Railroad controls Time.

I made it stand still.

The masses waited below with held breath to see if it was possible, if the Railroad could actually kill their elephant dead for them.

I smiled. A reassuring smile. You can depend on the Railroad.

I placed my hand on the hanging lever.

I gripped the handle hard, tasting the silent seconds, rolling them around in my mouth, knowing that this part, the before part, would be the best part of all.

And then I threw the lever.

And Time started up again.

(All gasp.)

The crane groaned, gears grinding and –

MARSHAL. Damn! If that thing don't lift off the ground! An elephant, for Pete's sake!

MUDDY TOWNSPERSON. It rose up steady till it was standin' on its hind legs, tiptoe. Toe nails scrapin' the railroad track. Tiptoe...like it was doin' a trick.

STEAM SHOVEL OPERATOR. Well, we started clappin' again, and I flashed a big smile down at Carl and them, 'cause they'd bet me there was no way in Hell that elephant was ever going to leave Mother Earth.

MARSHAL. But then we started wonderin' why that thing wasn't goin' any higher up.

YOUNG TOWNSPERSON. Gears sounded kinda stuck.

PREACHER. I got to thinkin' maybe she's too heavy, maybe a 100-ton crane can lift 100-ton steel but not a 5-ton animal. Maybe an elephant's soul is too heavy, maybe her soul is as heavy as the rest of her.

HUNGRY TOWNSPERSON. But that wasn't it.

ENGINEER. It wasn't the crane. Crane could lift her. Crane could lift her fine.

HUNGRY TOWNSPERSON. It was a people problem, not a crane problem. People don't always remember so good, even a big crowd of people, even thousands of people. People tend to not remember the little details when they got a elephant hangin' in front of them. And nobody did. Nobody remembered to unhook her. Nobody remembered she was still chained to the railroad track, her foot was still chained to the track.

STEAM SHOVEL OPERATOR. So they were kinda rippin' her in half a bit, pullin' her leg at this weird angle, her leg tryin' to hold her down to the ground while the rest of her was headed up.

MUDDY TOWNSPERSON. Her leg broke – a bone 'bout as big as my whole body – breakin', I could feel it in my spine, my spine buckled, ached in sympathy, rang like a tuning fork.

YOUNG TOWNSPERSON. Eli started cryin'.

STEAM SHOVEL OPERATOR. Shoulda left then, I s'pose.

YOUNG TOWNSPERSON. Eli ran off.

STEAM SHOVEL OPERATOR. But I stayed.

BALLET GIRL. Baby

STEAM SHOVEL OPERATOR. Stayed to see 'em unhook her foot, lift her up again –

BALLET GIRL. Baby

STEAM SHOVEL OPERATOR. – to see her trunk flailin' about, jerkin' around every which way, stabbin' the air like crazy, tryin' to grab hold of somethin'.

BALLET GIRL. Baby

PREACHER. Think she was nearly gone, then. Or woulda been, soon.

RINGMASTER. *(whispered)* No

PREACHER. That is…if the chain hadn't broke.

TOUR MANAGER & STRONGMAN. *(whispered)* No

PREACHER. But it broke.

BALLET GIRL & CLOWN. *(whispered)* No

PREACHER. The chain 'round her neck broke.

TRAINER. *(whispered)* No

ENGINEER. It wasn't the crane. Crane could lift her. Crane could lift her fine.

HUNGRY TOWNSPERSON. Mistake number two. It was a chain problem, not a crane problem. Chain 'round her neck couldn't handle all that weight. Weakest link, right?

YOUNG TOWNSPERSON. The chain popped and she came crashin' down onto the railroad track with this sound like an oak tree crackin' in half.

MUDDY TOWNSPERSON. She broke her…I think she broke her hip. Fight kinda went outta her. Couldn't seem to move, couldn't get off her side.

MARSHAL. It was loose.

PREACHER. Free.

YOUNG TOWNSPERSON. That little guy who climbed her before started screamin' like he was the one fell down and he yelled out to somebody and they handed him a thicker link chain and I couldn't believe it, but he ran up her back again.

PREACHER. Christ.

YOUNG TOWNSPERSON. His face was all red and twisted up, but – he just ran up there. Hooked her up again and ran off.

STEAM SHOVEL OPERATOR. Nobody clapped this time. Didn't seem…fact, some people started leavin', some of the women leadin' the kids off, anyway. Most stayed. I stayed. Stuck it out this far, I figured.

So

PREACHER. So

MARSHAL. So

MUDDY TOWNSPERSON. So

YOUNG TOWNSPERSON. So

HUNGRY TOWNSPERSON. So

MARSHAL. Crane lifted it off its feet again – higher…

YOUNG TOWNSPERSON. higher…

HUNGRY TOWNSPERSON. higher.

YOUNG TOWNSPERSON. She made some noises, some…air just kinda puffed outta her trunk and then that…that was it.

(Quiet.)

MUDDY TOWNSPERSON. I let my breath out.

I breathed in, lungs searchin' for that sanctified air. Waiting. Waiting to be made clean.

But the air…it tasted no different. It was flat and stale and rank.

They hung that thing for nothin'.

I still got mud on my shoes.

(The **MUDDY TOWNSPERSON** *disappears.)*

BALLET GIRL. Made that crane keep swinging her for twenty minutes longer than they had to. Townies were waiting for her to let loose a bellow, rip herself free. Something that big couldn't die, could it? Something that full of life? But she was long gone, history.

Looks like I …I might need some diamonds after all.

(The **BALLET GIRL** *disappears.)*

MARSHAL. Look. Look at that thing swing.

There are people in this here country that'll tell ya that we've become a small nation, a nation of little people with little dreams, staring at the ground 'stead o' the stars.

Well, look at what we done did here today and then tell me that this country is dyin'. Look at what happened here today in Erwin and then tell me there ain't no more dreamers. We hung a damn elephant today. An elephant. We made the impossible possible. So pack up your grip and go if you don't love this country, if you can't see the glory that surrounds you, if you want to stay in the mud. 'Cause this is America, damnit. And we can do anything we dream of. Anything at all.

(The **MARSHAL** *disappears.)*

STRONGMAN. It dangles her effortlessly

Taunting me

I could never lift her like that

I could never lift her

I tried once

Just to see

I couldn't do it

Not to any of them

Even little Mabel

Even the baby

But there she is

Swept off her feet

Our star

By that

It mocks me

It mocks me

It mocks me

(The **STRONGMAN** *disappears.)*

PREACHER. I'd forgot about the rest of 'em. Everybody forgot.

But once the crane set that poor beast down on the ground, her sisters came lumberin' back into the yard. Quiet. Reverential. Walked right through the thousands of people gathered 'round like we were invisible. Marched right up and stood over her. Opened their mouths and…their prayers didn't make a sound, but the air felt like it was…like it was movin', like it was tremblin'.

Them elephants bent down and …they caressed that Mary with their trunks, like they were soothin' her, calmin' her spirit. Payin' their last respects.

That man – that little man – he walked over to the biggest one of the mourners, petted her, whispered somethin' in one of those huge ears and led her out. Other elephants fell in behind, grabbin' the tail in front of 'em, walkin' off in a funeral recessional.

I fell in too, brought up the rear – best be gettin' home, gather my notes. Glow was gone. Had a feelin' it was gonna be crowded on Sunday.

(The **PREACHER** *disappears.)*

TRAINER. I'm red-lightin' myself.

I'll settle down somewhere, work at a zoo.

Don't really matter.

I'll get older and I'll die.

And that'll be it.

It's your show now, Shadrack.

My spark…is out.

(The **TRAINER** *disappears.)*

YOUNG TOWNSPERSON. Ma gave Eli and me a good switchin' that night.

Wasn't the worst part, though.

Worst part was the dreams.

(The **YOUNG TOWNSPERSON** *disappears.)*

TOUR MANAGER. Johnson City was in two days.

(The **ENGINEER** *and the* **TOUR MANAGER** *lock eyes for a moment. The* **ENGINEER** *snaps shut his pocket watch.)*

We'd be ready.

(The **ENGINEER** *and* **TOUR MANAGER** *disappear.)*

HUNGRY TOWNSPERSON. Elephants got those brains like traps, don't forget nothin'. All those peanuts they eat, maybe. People? People got short mem'ries. Let go of a mem'ry just as soon as you give it to 'em.

But not me. I eat peanuts. Stops it all from blurrin' together. All them colored boys led out to the yard must blur together somethin' fierce, 'cause nobody ever talks about how they hung colored boys in Erwin. They just talk about how they hung an elephant.

Damndest thing. Damndest thing.

Peanut?

(The **HUNGRY TOWNSPERSON** *disappears, leaving his peanuts behind.)*

CLOWN. Why…

Why did the elephant cross the road?

What did the banana say to the elephant?

How can ya tell if an elephant is sleeping?

Why did the elephant quit the circus?

How do ya make an elephant disappear?

(He picks up a shovel and digs Mary's grave.)

STEAM SHOVEL OPERATOR. Hey.

(The **CLOWN** *digs.)*

Hey!

(The **CLOWN** *digs.)*

Thick mud. Hard to bury a squirrel, much less a…

(The **CLOWN** *digs.)*

I got a steam shovel. I could dig the hole.

(The **CLOWN** *digs.)*

You hear? I could dig the hole!

(The **CLOWN** *digs.)*

Hey.

(The **CLOWN** *digs.)*

Hey!

(The **CLOWN** *digs.)*

That's what we got machines for in the first place, right? To help people? Make the job easier?

(The **CLOWN** *digs.)*

What?

(The **CLOWN** *digs.)*

What?

(The **CLOWN** *digs.)*

I could dig the hole! I could dig the hole! LET ME DIG THE HOLE!

(The **CLOWN** *stops digging. He rises, defiant tears streaming down his face.)*

Please.

(They stare at each other across the stage.
A moment.
Lights slowly fade on the two men and up on the **RING-MASTER.***
Train whistle.)

RINGMASTER. It was September and there was a Town and there was a Circus and there was a Railroad and there was a Man with Red Hair and there was an Elephant.
There was an Elephant

RINGMASTER. *(cont.)* An Elephant

—

You pack up the tent
You load the boxcars

You wait

You wait

After midnight, after the townsfolk have gone home
after the prying eyes of Erwin are closed
safe

safe

safe and asleep in their beds
sleeping with the certainty that their boogie monster
is dead
good and dead
that they can get on with their stupid worthless lives in
their stupid worthless town in their stupid worthless...

You wake up the Clowns.

You wake up the Clowns and put the shovels back in
their hands.
You tell them to dig her up.

You tell them to dig her up and saw off her tusks.
You tell them to saw off her tusks and you tell them to
bring them to you.

You have to see what you can salvage, what you can get
for them, for the ivory, the tusks.

An elephant is an investment.

*(Sound of the steam train struggling to life. Lights fade
on the broken* **RINGMASTER** *as the train sound builds,
ending with a long and lonesome whistle.)*

End of Play

ABOUT THE PLAYWRIGHT

GEORGE BRANT's plays include *Any Other Name, Elephant's Graveyard, Ashes, NOK, The Lonesome Hoboes, One Hand Clapping, Terminal One, The Royal Historian of Oz, Lovely Letters, Three Men in a Boat, Borglum! The Mount Rushmore Musical, Tights on a Wire* and *Night of the Mime.* His work has been produced and developed by Trinity Repertory Company, the Kennedy Center, the Playwrights Foundation, Capitol Hill Arts Center, the Playwrights' Center, WordBRIDGE Playwright's Lab, ATHE, Premiere Stages, Trustus Theatre, Balagan Theatre, Open Fist Theatre Company, Theatre 4, Perishable Theatre, the Drama League, the Disney Channel, Circle Theatre, Factory Theatre, Street-Signs Theatre Company, Prop Thtr, Hyde Park Theatre, the Guerrilla Shakespeare Project and zeppo theater company. His script *Elephant's Graveyard* was awarded the David Mark Cohen National Playwriting Award from the Kennedy Center and the Keene Prize for Literature. He has received writing fellowships from the James A. Michener Center for Writers, the MacDowell Colony, and the Blue Mountain Center. George received his Masters in Writing from the University of Texas at Austin and is a member of the Dramatists Guild.

OTHER TITLES AVAILABLE FROM SAMUEL FRENCH

SONG OF EXTINCTION

EM Lewis

Drama / 5m, 1f

A play about the science of life and loss, the relationships between fathers and sons, Cambodian fields, Bolivian rainforests and redemption. Max Forrestal is going to fail Biology if he doesn't complete a 20-page paper on extinction by 2pm on Tuesday — but his mother, Lily, is dying of cancer, and school is the last thing on his mind. His father, Ellery, a biologist obsessed with saving a rare Bolivian insect, is incapable of dealing with his wife's impending death, or his son's distress. Max's biology teacher, Khim Phan, tries to figure out why Max is failing the class. Helping Max, however, pushes Khim into a magical journey of his own — from the Cambodian fields of his youth into the undiscovered country beyond.

**2009 Harold and Mimi Steinberg/ATCA New Play Award
— American Theater Critics Association**

2008 Ted Schmitt Award for the world premiere of an Outstanding New Play – Los Angeles Drama Critics Circle

**2008 Production of the Year — The LA Weekly Awards
– Los Angeles, CA**

2009 University of Oregon EcoDrama Festival Winner

2008 Ashland New Plays Festival Winner

"CRITIC'S CHOICE...Artfully balances its theme of mortality between the intimate and the macroscopic...explores inner psychological states with remarkable eloquence and clarity."
- The Los Angeles Times

"GO!...The interplay of the three [views on extinction] in Lewis' smart and honest script is one small push away from collective transcendence."
- LA Weekly

OTHER TITLES AVAILABLE FROM SAMUEL FRENCH

SECRET GARDEN - SPRING VERSION

Book and Lyrics by Marsha Norman
Music by Lucy Simon
Based on the novel by Frances Hodgson Burnett

Musical / 8m, 7f, 1f child, 1m child, Chorus / Unit Set
The long-awaited new 70-minute version of the beloved musical is as beautiful and spirited as the original in just half the time. Adapted by Marsha Norman from her Tony-award winning book, it tells the story of Mary Lennox, orphaned in India, who returns to Yorkshire to live with an embittered, reclusive uncle and his invalid son. On the estate, she discovers a locked garden filled with magic, a boy who talks to birds, and a cousin she brings back to health by putting him to work in the garden. The original chorus of ghosts has been replaced with a chorus of Readers, who sit onstage and watch the musical unfold before their eyes, singing in most scenes, and even participating as desired in the storm scene at the end of the first act, and the frolic in the Night Garden. Lucy Simon's music, some of the most beautiful ever written for Broadway, has made this tale of regeneration a favorite for almost 20 years. This new Spring version promises to be a treasure for children and adults.

www.ingramcontent.com/pod-product-compliance
Lightning Source LLC
Chambersburg PA
CBHW070421120726
47909CB00005B/1744